Samuel French Acting Edition

I0591984

Welcome to the White Room

by Trish Harnetiaux

SAMUELFRENCH.COM   SAMUELFRENCH.CO.UK

FOR PRODUCTION ENQUIRIES

UNITED STATES AND CANADA
Info@SamuelFrench.com
1-866-598-8449

UNITED KINGDOM AND EUROPE
Plays@SamuelFrench.co.uk
020-7255-4302

Each title is subject to availability from Samuel French, depending upon country of performance. Please be aware that *WELCOME TO THE WHITE ROOM* may not be licensed by Samuel French in your territory. Professional and amateur producers should contact the nearest Samuel French office or licensing partner to verify availability.

MUSIC USE NOTE

Licensees are solely responsible for obtaining formal written permission from copyright owners to use copyrighted music in the performance of this play and are strongly cautioned to do so. If no such permission is obtained by the licensee, then the licensee must use only original music that the licensee owns and controls. Licensees are solely responsible and liable for all music clearances and shall indemnify the copyright owners of the play(s) and their licensing agent, Samuel French, against any costs, expenses, losses and liabilities arising from the use of music by licensees. Please contact the appropriate music licensing authority in your territory for the rights to any incidental music.

IMPORTANT BILLING AND CREDIT REQUIREMENTS

If you have obtained performance rights to this title, please refer to your licensing agreement for important billing and credit requirements.

WELCOME TO THE WHITE ROOM was first produced by Lynn Morton at Glass Mind Theatre in Baltimore, Maryland on November 14, 2014. The performance was directed by Chris Cotterman, with set design by Michelle Datz, light and sound design and composition by Brad J. Ranno, costume design by Stephanie Parks, prop design by Kate Smith-Morse, dialect coaching by Ann Turiano, and choreography by Jessica Ruth Baker. The production manager was Jesse Herche and the production stage manager was Kate Smith-Morse. The cast was as follows:

MS. WHITE . . . . Jessica Ruth Baker

MR. PAINE. . . . . Eric Park

JENNINGS. . . . . Kevin Griffin Moreno

PATRICK . . . . Justin Lawson Isett

CHARACTERS

MS. WHITE – a pretty, sultry woman in her thirties
MR. PAINE – a slightly awkward, easily distracted man in his forties
JENNINGS – a British type in his fifties
PATRICK – a video-gaming boy-man in his twenties

SETTING

The entire play takes place in The White Room.

TIME

The time is Now.

AUTHOR'S NOTES

Diverse casting is more than encouraged.

The titles for each section should be projected at the start of that section.

"How could they see anything but the shadows if they were never allowed to move their heads?"

– *Plato*, Allegory of the Cave

PART ONE – THE WHITE ROOM

(The room is completely white. There is a door with a slot upstage. **MS. WHITE**, **MR. PAINE**, *and* **JENNINGS** *are standing staring at each other. They are all wearing white coats and each carries a bag. There is a small pedestal in the middle of the room. They have just arrived.)*

MS. WHITE. Ms. White.

MR. PAINE. Ah, Ms. White.

JENNINGS. Ms. White.

MS. WHITE. You…

JENNINGS. Jennings.

MS. WHITE. Jennings.

MR. PAINE. Ah, Jennings. Mr. Paine.

MS. WHITE. Mr. Paine.

JENNINGS. Mr. Paine, your reputation precedes you.

MR. PAINE. As does yours.

MS. WHITE. And yours.

MR. PAINE. And yours.

JENNINGS. And yours.

MS. WHITE. And yours.

> *(Beat.)*

Who will start?

JENNINGS. Mr. Paine?

MS. WHITE. Mr. Paine?

MR. PAINE. Ms. White.

JENNINGS. Ms. White.

MS. WHITE. Very well.

JENNINGS. We don't have much time –

MS. WHITE. – I'll be quick –

MR. PAINE. – It's part of it all.

MS. WHITE. I think we're being timed.

MR. PAINE. We're being timed.

MS. WHITE. I'm sure of it.

JENNINGS. One minute each.

MR. PAINE. Reasonable.

JENNINGS. Very.

MR. PAINE. Go.

MS. WHITE. I was a child genius. Not immediately identifiable at first –

MR. PAINE. Never is.

JENNINGS. Never is.

MS. WHITE. There was something special about me. I saw things, things others didn't. By the time I was five I understood: action, reaction, displacement, geometry, parallelograms, pi, hyperbola, refraction, reflection, retraction, the cortex, the cerebellum, the function of the frontal lobe, neurotransmitters and nanotechnology.

At six I had mocked up the entire solar system – to scale – in my bedroom.

I've been cultivating this, and I know that with it, with this knowledge, comes a certain responsibility. I assume we all have one – to impact and leave a mark, not a scratch or a bruise, but a big, red gash-of-a-mark. A pretty mark. A helpful mark. A big red mark. But a mark no less. I've known since I was a small, tiny, child genius.

JENNINGS. Out with it.

MS. WHITE. Of course.

> *(Takes her bag off her shoulder and removes The Device.)*

Careful.

> *(She sets it on the small pedestal.)*

MR. PAINE. Impressive.

MS. WHITE. Thank you.

MR. PAINE. Jennings?

JENNINGS. Impressive.

MR. PAINE. Ms. White –

MS. WHITE. Mr. Paine?

MR. PAINE. Does it convert?

MS. WHITE. Of course, they all convert these days –

JENNINGS. Transform?

MS. WHITE. Both converts and transforms.

JENNINGS. The objective?

MS. WHITE. Less objective, more subjective.

MR. PAINE. Excellent.

MS. WHITE. I thought so. It changes on touch, varies from player to player, senses through pressure the exact way in which to unfold, convert, and transform.

MR. PAINE. The outcome?

MS. WHITE. It varies.

JENNINGS. Obviously.

MS. WHITE. Yes.

JENNINGS. Paine – touch it.

MS. WHITE. Yes, touch it.

MR. PAINE. Alright.

> (**MR. PAINE** *reaches out and touches The Device. He stands motionless with his hand on it. His legs begin to shake, his eyes close. He begins humming.*)

JENNINGS. Incredible.

MS. WHITE. Just wait…

> (**MR. PAINE** *begins to cluck like a chicken.* **MS. WHITE** *circles him as she speaks.*)

Upon touch, he is instantly sent into a state of REM – hence the flickers and the jitters. But what his entire body, not just his mind, is actually experiencing is RBM – Rapid Body Movement. Each muscle is reliving a memory, an experience. Normally, muscles during REM are paralyzed, but I have reversed the experience through The Device and the body now fully embraces and acts out what the mind is seeing.

> (**MR. PAINE** *begins sputtering words but remains in a shaking state of full-bodied RBM mode.*)

JENNINGS. How long does it last?

MR. PAINE. KILL! KILL!

MS. WHITE. It is designed to "run its course."

MR. PAINE. KILL!

MS. WHITE. These sudden outbursts are a direct result of what Mr. Paine is experiencing. They are traditionally the second stage – there are three – of what we call FULL EXPERIENCE. He is having what I would diagnose as a very eventful and healthy ride.

MR. PAINE. GRAB THE PURPLE ROPE!

> (**MS. WHITE** *laughs, amused.*)

GRAB THE PURPLE ROPE!

JENNINGS. Amusing?

MS. WHITE. This purple rope. It's common, people often see the purple rope.

MR. PAINE. GRAB THE PURPLE ROPE!

MS. WHITE. Personally, I have never seen it.

JENNINGS. And the third stage of Full Experience?

MS. WHITE. Wait…

> (**MR. PAINE** *resumes the chicken clucking briefly.*)

On target, there is a slight digression and dip back to the first image, then –

> (**MR. PAINE**'s *body goes into full spastic mode, his sounds build to a climactic yodel, and he collapses to the ground, out.*)

JENNINGS. Will he remember it?

MS. WHITE. Yes, some of it.

JENNINGS. How long until he's up?

MS. WHITE. Five, four, three, two –

> (**MR. PAINE** *sits straight up, gasping for air.*)

One.

JENNINGS. Paine, does it hurt?

MR. PAINE. Glorious.

> *(Gasp.)*

Ms. White, glorious. Bravo.

MS. WHITE. Did you grab the purple rope?

MR. PAINE. *Did I grab the purple rope.* I rode the purple rope up the mountain, over the desert, there was water, then I was swimming and I saw this fish. It swam by me and part of its fin was missing. Something incredibly violent had happened. Like a huge shark had taken a bite out of it with its sharp shark teeth. It swam in this slow, lethargic way and its eye – just one of them – rolled over and looked at me – the fish was just staring at me – and then his little fish mouth mouthed the word CAUTION and he swam off.

I was on my way to…something, somewhere, but was –

JENNINGS. Sucked out?

MR. PAINE. – sucked out, yes.

MS. WHITE. You ran out of time.

MR. PAINE. Must have.

JENNINGS. Minute's up, White.

MS. WHITE. Jennings, you go, Mr. Paine might need to catch his breath.

JENNINGS. Of course.

MR. PAINE. The purple rope…

JENNINGS. I will make this very fast –

MR. PAINE. I am a very fast listener.

MS. WHITE. As am I –

JENNINGS. – we need to move it along.

MS. WHITE. So speak as fast as you can and we will listen even faster.

MR. PAINE. Even faster.

JENNINGS. Brilliant.

> (*JENNINGS removes The Apparatus from his bag and sets it next to The Device on the pedestal. He speaks very fast.*)

A minimum of two players are necessary. Opponents. An archaic term sure, but The Apparatus feeds off opposing energy and long term strategy.

If it is attempted to be played by a sole player, just one, they would lose, and lose to No One – since "No One" will eventually win out over Someone. "No One" has the advantage. "No One" will not be tempted to make the wrong decision or, god forbid, to follow their heart. "No One" obviously will win, so two must play.

Ms. White, hold this.

> (*Hands her Player A stick of The Apparatus, hands Player B to* **MR. PAINE.***)

Mr. Paine. When I say go, you must GO. Immediately. You must immediately go. Ready, set, GO.

> (*They simply stand there.*)

Are you going?

MR. PAINE. I'm going, Ms. White?

MS. WHITE. Yes, I'm going too.

JENNINGS. Excellent. Now – let's speed it up – you will feel vibrations on the stick. One vibration means turn left, two right, three backwards, four forwards, five down, six up and so on. Understood?

MS. WHITE. Understood.

MR. PAINE. Understood.

> (*JENNINGS pushes a button on The Apparatus. They both begin twisting and turning, responding to the vibrations from The Apparatus. Then they are still.*)

JENNINGS. Mr. Paine, congratulations.

MS. WHITE. He won?

MR. PAINE. I won!

JENNINGS. Clearly Mr. Paine won, and won proper, proper won. He anticipated each movement and well ahead of you, Ms. White.

MR. PAINE. Clearly.

MS. WHITE. Are you sure?

MR. PAINE. Ms. White, I think it's clear.

JENNINGS. Perhaps next time.

MR. PAINE. Next time.

JENNINGS. Minute's up. Paine?

MR. PAINE. Yes.

> *(He retrieves The Mechanism from his bag. It is impossibly small, invisible actually. He sets it next to The Device and The Apparatus on the pedestal.)*

Wait.

> *(They wait.)*

Ms. White?

MS. WHITE. Wisconsin.

MR. PAINE. Good. Jennings?

JENNINGS. Cashmere.

MR. PAINE. Correct. White?

MS. WHITE. Charlemagne.

MR. PAINE. Yes.

JENNINGS. El Cid.

MR. PAINE. So easy!

MS. WHITE. Zirconium.

MR. PAINE. Yes.

JENNINGS. The Orange.

MR. PAINE. No – Ms. White?

MS. WHITE. The Apple!

MR. PAINE. Correct. Sorry Jennings, Ms. White – congratulations.

MS. WHITE. Genius.

JENNINGS. Nice work, Paine.

MR. PAINE. Thank you. Over ten years in the creation.

JENNINGS. Well worth it, mate.

MR. PAINE. That was only level one. The Mechanism has infinite levels.

JENNINGS. Indeed.

MS. WHITE. Satellite?

JENNINGS. Waves?

MS. WHITE. No need to reveal, Paine. They have selected well.

JENNINGS. The three of us.

MS. WHITE. Yes.

MR. PAINE. Agreed.

MS. WHITE. Agreed.

JENNINGS. A pleasure.

MS. WHITE. Should we start?

> *(Beat.)*

MR. PAINE. At once.

MS. WHITE. Do you have the instructions?

MR. PAINE. Instructions?

JENNINGS. Instructions?

MS. WHITE. Instructions.

JENNINGS. No. Paine?

MR. PAINE. No –

> *(Suddenly, a red envelope is thrust through the slot in the door. They all turn to stare.)*

PART TWO – THE SLOT IN THE DOOR TO THE WHITE ROOM

(**MS. WHITE** *opens the letter.*)

MS. WHITE. Welcome To The White Room,

The three of you are here because you are the elite, the best of the best. You have been handpicked, handmade and hand destined to aid – perhaps even solve – the most coveted and desirable game that has ever existed.

The objectives are simple: assess, deduce, implement, and apply. The key to achieving success is teamwork – and this will only be accomplished if you work together as a team.

Every skill is needed, every notion useful.

As guessed, you are being timed and will be rewarded for swiftness and efficiency. You each possess a specific quality that is necessary, so do not discount anything. Remember, you will need to tap into your untapped potential, your inner instinct and fuse ideas.

Good luck.

MR. PAINE. That's it?

JENNINGS. I hate that "good luck."

MS. WHITE. Strange.

JENNINGS. What a terrible thing to say.

MR. PAINE. It's an expression of good will, Jennings.

JENNINGS. It's implying that bad luck is inherent.

MS. WHITE. Inherent?

JENNINGS. To life, to breathing, to luck.

MR. PAINE. Jennings, don't talk about luck, there is no luck. You – of all people should know that –

JENNINGS. Which is precisely why this "good luck" is so awful. The very concept – disturbing. Makes me sad actually.

MS. WHITE. That's not possible.

JENNINGS. Makes me feel – that I am an animal. I actively feel like an animal.

MR. PAINE. You look like a boar Jennings, you could be a boar?

JENNINGS. And, they've given no clue where to start.

MS. WHITE. Perhaps that is the clue itself.

MR. PAINE. The negative, yes.

MS. WHITE. The clue is in the letter.

    (Beat.)

JENNINGS. Which of us is the decoder?

MS. WHITE. Not I.

MR. PAINE. KILL! KILL!

MS. WHITE. *My Lord.*

JENNINGS. What just happened.

MS. WHITE. It happens on occasion. It'll wear off –

JENNINGS. Ms. White, are they aware of the defect?

MS. WHITE. It's not a defect –

MR. PAINE. KILL!

MS. WHITE. Merely a continuation.

JENNINGS. A continuation?

MS. WHITE. While technically Mr. Paine's time with The Device is over, there is a slight, a slight residue if you will –

MR. PAINE. KILL!

    (Hiccups.)

Pardon me.

MS. WHITE. It should pass.

MR. PAINE. Do you know what has just happened?

MS. WHITE. What happened.

MR. PAINE. It's…my hair, it's ever so slightly in my face.

JENNINGS. Obstructing your vision is it?

MR. PAINE. Yes, but before I noticed it, I clearly remember being on…on a…brink.

MS. WHITE. I love brinks!

MR. PAINE. There was very clear imagery… And I was – I was…

JENNINGS. You were on the brink, Paine.

MR. PAINE. Yes. Everything's a bit fuzzy now.

MS. WHITE. Hazy?

MR. PAINE. Both fuzzy and hazy.

JENNINGS. Should we cut it, Paine?

MS. WHITE. Cut the hair?

JENNINGS. Should we cut the hair?

MR. PAINE. A haircut?

JENNINGS. It won't hurt, Paine.

MR. PAINE. Are there scissors?

MS. WHITE. Can we cut hair?

JENNINGS. I bet Ms. White can nip off your hairs one by one with those sharp little teeth of hers –

MS. WHITE. They are sharp –

JENNINGS. They're like fox teeth, I bet foxes just go around with these sharp little teeth that are exactly like Ms. White's teeth –

MR. PAINE. But who had the teeth first, Ms. White or the Fox?

JENNINGS. Perhaps Ms. White is in fact the Fox.

MR. PAINE. Clever Jennings, I like it.

MS. WHITE. If Jennings is a boar, I could be a fox…

MR. PAINE. Wait, watch, I can just take my hands and use them as combs through my hair, comb them through my hair, then take this small, renegade part here, and tuck it like this, just behind my ear.

MS. WHITE. How's your brink, Paine?

MR. PAINE. It's…better, I think my brink is coming back!

(**MS. WHITE** *hands the letter to* **MR. PAINE.**)

MS. WHITE. What do you see?

MR. PAINE. I may have a brink, but I am certainly not a decoder.

MS. WHITE. Read it.

MR. PAINE. It's blank.

JENNINGS. Blank.

MR. PAINE. Ms. White, you must have handed me the wrong letter.

MS. WHITE. Impossible.

MR. PAINE. I'm not lying, Ms. White.

JENNINGS. Let me see.

MR. PAINE. Here.

JENNINGS. Blank.

MS. WHITE. Blank. Huh. If the ink was time-sensitive, it could have been distinguishable for moments only. We need to hurry –

JENNINGS. – She's right –

MS. WHITE. – we need to start. Somewhere, with something. Mr. Paine – what are you thinking?

MR. PAINE. Thinking?

JENNINGS. Thinking, Paine!

MR. PAINE. Origin. The letter mentioned something about each of us, personally, it knows us, we can start there. With instinct.

MS. WHITE. Excellent.

MR. PAINE. My instinct… Wait… This is a bit, a bit unusual –

MS. WHITE. – Out with it –

MR. PAINE. My instinct is to…kiss Ms. White.

MS. WHITE. What?

(**JENNINGS** *laughs.*)

JENNINGS. Nice one, Paine.

MR. PAINE. *(With gaining momentum.)* It is, I feel it, here. My lips. They are burning ever so lightly. My body is listing in your direction, Ms. White, I can't stop it. See?

Look how my legs are slanted slightly, how my arm inexplicably reaches toward you... I feel I should act – ignite a spark in us all. Jennings, turn around –

MS. WHITE. This is absu –

JENNINGS. I'm watching, Paine. If you're going to kiss Ms. White, the least I can do is watch you do it. I feel that, here, must be my instinct.

MS. WHITE. Your inner-animal Jennings?

JENNINGS. Exactly, my inner-animal.

MR. PAINE. Fact – when an ovulating female boar is exposed to a pheromone from a male boar's saliva, the scent travels along the olfactory nerve directly into the amygdala, stimulating the release of neurotransmitters, the result of which is that she becomes immediately and completely paralyzed in a spread-legged mating posture!

MS. WHITE. Mr. Paine, your facts are in order, but I fail to see how this will help –

MR. PAINE. Perhaps, yes, the boars, maybe it's not limited to them, we too could end up –

JENNINGS. – In a spread-legged mating posture? This is all good, very good, progress is being made. THIS is why we're here. They're not dumb – they knew we'd start with instinct instead of fodder.

MS. WHITE. Fodder?

JENNINGS. Everything is fodder these days, rarely is there instinct.

MR. PAINE. I'm listing, Ms. White... Do you see how I lean for you?

JENNINGS. Let's think about this.

Say you kiss Ms. White. Then what? Sure, momentarily you are sent into orbit, eyes closed, lips wet, head spinning, unsure if your feet are still on the ground – thinking perhaps the two of you now occupy a different plane from the rest of reality – that you've finally found it, made it, are in a state of existence that catapults you above and beyond the rest of normal civilization and its celestial counterparts...

But wait...what then...what's this? Once you've drawn apart and your eyes have left each other, what then I ask?

I'll tell you what, Paine: coldness, darkness.

Ms. White will quietly turn away as she thinks fondly, only, of the first time she was kissed on the playground when she was a small child genius of six, how the boy's hand had lingered on her child waist just long enough to plant a taste of what's to come in her child brain.

You'll have sudden flashes of ex-wives and satin sheets, your mind already horizontal, hovering above reason and clouded in the moment, not to clear until another front storms in and wipes away all memory of what it felt like to float for just one moment in time, to fly.

And both of you, and this will only take seconds, will be deflated, dulled and de-mystified by all the power held in the suggestion of the kiss, the kinetic transcendency of what could be – but dashed by what was.

> (**MR. PAINE**, *who had been listing and leaning toward* **MS. WHITE** *through* **JENNINGS**' *speech, slowly rights himself to a normal standing position. They are silent for a moment.*)

MR. PAINE. Quite a mouthful, Jennings.

JENNINGS. I'm trained to think ahead.

MR. PAINE. I see.

MS. WHITE. There's something to what you've said. This idea that there is a form of kinetic energy that is perhaps, what's the word – harvestable? – in the moment before a kiss.

MR. PAINE. What?

MS. WHITE. I'm saying your instinct to kiss me was right, but as Jennings noted – the instinct was right because we're looking for that energy and inspiration. We need to channel the energy, not use it up on useless kissing.

MR. PAINE. Useless kissing?

MS. WHITE. Think about it.

> (**MR. PAINE** *thinks about it.*)

MR. PAINE. Useless?

JENNINGS. I'm following you White –

MS. WHITE. *(With growing excitement.)* Dopamine, neurotransmitters, pleasure receptors – all are affected during the kiss. Jennings, I see where you're going –

JENNINGS. The actual act has been thought of as the equivalent of –

MS. WHITE. Bungee jumping –

JENNINGS. Parachuting –

MR. PAINE. Adrenaline… Yes, you're right.

> (*Smacking his head.*)

Idiot. Of course, we're being timed, the pressure's on, my longing –

JENNINGS. – and listing –

MS. WHITE. – and leaning –

MR. PAINE. – for Ms. White – is all part of the plan to get us to the ideal state of creative epiphany.

MS. WHITE. It's so…raw.

MR. PAINE. And flawed.

JENNINGS. Almost dirty –

> (*Suddenly, a package is thrust through the slot in the door. They all turn to stare.*)

PART THREE – THE PACKAGE THAT CAME THROUGH THE SLOT IN THE DOOR TO THE WHITE ROOM

(MS. WHITE, MR. PAINE, *and* JENNINGS *are staring at the package.*)

MS. WHITE. Not it.

JENNINGS. Not it.

MR. PAINE. Not it.

JENNINGS. We said it before you.

MR. PAINE. Not it. I said it twice.

JENNINGS. Not it.

MR. PAINE. Ms. White.

MS. WHITE. Mr. Paine. The last person to say Not It is IT. And it's you.

MR. PAINE. But, I said it –

MS. WHITE. It doesn't work that way.

MR. PAINE. Fine.

(*He picks up the package and opens it. There are three votive candles, a book of matches, and a negligee.*)

Ms. White, it seems to be for you.

MS. WHITE. Is there a note?

(*He shakes the package and a note falls out.*)

Read it.

MR. PAINE. It's blank. Jennings.

(*Hands note to* JENNINGS.)

JENNINGS. Blank.

(*Hands note to* MS. WHITE.)

Ms. White.

MS. WHITE. It's not blank.

JENNINGS. (*Amused.*) You have a power.

MS. WHITE. Nonsense.

JENNINGS. They have given you a power. You can read it.

MR. PAINE. She doesn't have a power.

MS. WHITE. Of course I can read it.

MR. PAINE. We don't have powers –

MS. WHITE. *(Reading from the letter.)* As you can see by now, Ms. White has a power. She can see messages that you two can not. Powers may out themselves along the way, you are rewarded as well as penalized for your actions throughout the course.

You've passed the test of The Kiss, nice work, Jennings. From here you must take what you've learned and start towards the final stretch and goal.

Your next task is to bring back the three-dimensional pastimes. This here –

> *(Through the slot in the door comes The Last Deck of Cards in the World – it lands with a thud.)*

– is The Last Deck of Cards in the World. Since the digitalization of all games, it has remained hidden in the hills of –

MR. PAINE. GRAB THE PURPLE ROPE!

MS. WHITE. – the hills of THE HILL. It is now in your hands to guide you in your mission. Use it wisely.

> *(MR. PAINE is moving toward The Device on the pedestal. JENNINGS blocks his path.)*

JENNINGS. Ms. White –

MS. WHITE. Let him go! The Device has been known to summon a player back in to contribute to the FULL EXPERIENCE. It was designed this way…

JENNINGS. Are you sure –

MS. WHITE. Instinct Jennings, we have to just allow what is happening to happen.

JENNINGS. Mr. Paine. MISTER PAINE!

> *(JENNINGS picks up The Last Deck of Cards in the World and offers it to MR. PAINE.)*

Game of cards, Paine?

MR. PAINE. *(Broken of his desire to reach The Device.)* A deck of cards.

> *(Beat.)*

Four suits, four seasons – fifty-two cards, fifty-two weeks in a year – thirteen cards per suit, thirteen phases of a lunar cycle. If you add up the value of every single card and add one for the joker – you get 365 – the days of the year. A deck of cards makes perfect sense.

MS. WHITE. Mr. Paine, are you alright?

MR. PAINE. The last time I saw a deck of cards I was on a dock. It was during The Big Clean; they had come by boat during the night to take them. I had woken up knowing they were in the house, making noise downstairs –

MS. WHITE. – Mr. Paine –

MR. PAINE. We had had chicken for dinner that night. Chicken with noodles and broccoli. I'd broccoli in the back of my teeth –

> *(Trying to remove it with his tongue during the following.)*

I didn't brush – went in and turned the water on – made some noises – spat a few times, but never brushed.

> *(Then normal.)*

I thought it was the cat at first, the noises –

MS. WHITE. Jennings…

MR. PAINE. – and I snuck down the staircase. I knew that if I sat on the third stair from the bottom and looked at the family portrait on the wall I could see the entire living room in the reflection. So I waited…

JENNINGS. Go on, Paine…

MR. PAINE. I didn't know what I was seeing at first… The black robes, the foreign tongue. I watched as they took every one of them. The trivia games, the balls, the jacks, the Hungry, Hungry Hippos, the coloring box – everything. I thought they'd missed it, I thought they were going to leave me at least that – but then they reached the last drawer and took all of my cards.

> *(He has opened the pack of cards and is fanning through them.)*

Look! The Jack of Spades, my favorite card.

JENNINGS. Why the Jack, Paine?

MR. PAINE. He's young and powerful.

> *(Beat.)*

Let's play war.

MS. WHITE. We should be careful –

MR. PAINE. Best of ten hands, White – I win, you put on the dress.

MS. WHITE. And if I win?

MR. PAINE. I'll put on the dress.

MS. WHITE. Deal.

MR. PAINE. Jennings, care to shuffle.

JENNINGS. Why not.

> *(He shuffles the cards like a professional dealer.)*

I have never… I did not know I could shuffle this well.

MR. PAINE. You're excellent.

JENNINGS. Are we worried about time?

MS. WHITE. This oddly feels right…

JENNINGS. Thought so.

MS. WHITE. But hurry.

JENNINGS. Here you go.

> **(MR. PAINE** *takes the deck and gives half to* **MS. WHITE.***)*

MR. PAINE. Okay, go.

> *(They both flip a card over.)*

Ace of Spades.

MS. WHITE. Two. Damn.

MR. PAINE. Again.

(Flip.)

MR. PAINE. *(Cont.)* King of Spades.

MS. WHITE. Three.

MR. PAINE. Again.

(Flip.)

Queen of Spades!

MS. WHITE. Four. Your deck's rigged, Mr. Paine.

MR. PAINE. Keep it up! Again.

(Flip.)

The Jack of Spades!

MS. WHITE. Five.

MR. PAINE. What's the score, Jennings?

JENNINGS. One more and Ms. White's in the dress.

MR. PAINE. Again.

(Flip.)

Ten of Spades!

MS. WHITE. No – my card was the Ten of Spades.

MR. PAINE. Ridiculous, that there is my card.

MS. WHITE. Mine.

MR. PAINE. *(Holding card up.)* Mine.

> **(MS. WHITE** *grabs the card too; they are both holding it.)*

MS. WHITE. Mine.

MR. PAINE. Mine.

MS. WHITE. Mine.

MR. PAINE. Mine.

JENNINGS. Children!

> *(They rip the card in half. There is a shocked silence.)*

MS. WHITE. I can't believe you did –

MR. PAINE. You did it!

MS. WHITE. You did it!

JENNINGS. Stop it!

> *(He grabs both halves of the card and shoves them into his mouth. He speaks while chewing.)*

Now it's mine.

MS. WHITE. *(Picking up the Jack of Spades.)* Let's see how tasty your precious Jack of Spades is.

> *(She puts it in her mouth and starts chewing it.)*

MR. PAINE. Stop!

> *(**MS. WHITE** and **JENNINGS** continue chewing. At a loss, **MR. PAINE** grabs a card and starts chewing it as well. Throughout the following they eat The Last Deck of Cards in the World.)*

JENNINGS. Not bad actually...

MR. PAINE. Good.

MS. WHITE. Quite good.

MR. PAINE. What does yours taste like?

MS. WHITE. Veal?

JENNINGS. Yes, veal. I hadn't realized how hungry I was.

MS. WHITE. Nor I.

JENNINGS. This one's got a bit of broccoli bits in it.

MS. WHITE. Which is it?

JENNINGS. A Heart.

> *(**MS. WHITE** eats a Heart.)*

MS. WHITE. You're right –

JENNINGS. Delicious.

MR. PAINE. Do you think –

JENNINGS. – that this is bad?

MR. PAINE. Perhaps.

JENNINGS. Can't see how, they gave us the deck, and why would they do that if we were NOT supposed to eat it.

MS. WHITE. It was the Last Deck –

MR. PAINE. – the Last Deck.

MS. WHITE. In the Whole World.

JENNINGS. Perhaps that's why they're so good. Try a Heart with a Club, sandwiched with another Heart –

MR. PAINE. Amazing.

MS. WHITE. Grab a Spade, fold a Diamond in half, and put another Spade on it –

MR. PAINE. Ms. White –

JENNINGS. It's like chocolate.

MR. PAINE. Chocolate!

JENNINGS. Ms. White – try this bit of chocolate.

MS. WHITE. Delicious.

>(MR. PAINE*'s arm begins to slowly rise. Throughout his exchange with* JENNINGS, MS. WHITE *continues to eat the rest of the cards.)*

JENNINGS. Look at your arm.

MR. PAINE. I know. What is it doing?

JENNINGS. Hmm.

MR. PAINE. Why do you think it's doing that?

JENNINGS. Perhaps it prefers to be up.

MR. PAINE. Ah.

JENNINGS. Yes.

MR. PAINE. Yes.

JENNINGS. Higher. Clearly your arm prefers some height.

MR. PAINE. I think you're right.

JENNINGS. It's quite interesting actually, the way it keeps rising like that –

MR. PAINE. It's almost flapping now, isn't it.

JENNINGS. Quite.

MR. PAINE. Do you think…no.

JENNINGS. What?

MR. PAINE. That I could possibly…

JENNINGS. Fly?

MR. PAINE. Yes! Do you think so?

JENNINGS. No, impossible.

MR. PAINE. Thought not.

JENNINGS. Sorry, Paine.

MR. PAINE. It was just that... It seemed, the arm, it seemed the arm *wanted to fly*.

JENNINGS. It's what they call a "shame" I believe.

MR. PAINE. It's a shame for sure.

JENNINGS. Shame about the arm – they'd say.

MR. PAINE. Shame you can't fly.

JENNINGS. Shame you can't fly – they'd say.

MR. PAINE. Shame on me.

JENNINGS. Good one, Paine, shame on you.

MR. PAINE. It seems to be slowing now.

JENNINGS. Perhaps the arm is tired.

MR. PAINE. It might be, that makes sense.

JENNINGS. Sense?

MR. PAINE. The arm, slowing, tired, sense.

JENNINGS. Yes, sense.

MR. PAINE. Ms. White's been rather quiet hasn't she.

JENNINGS. She has.

MR. PAINE. Indeed.

JENNINGS. Ms. White?

MR. PAINE. Do you think there could be any reason that she could no longer see us?

MS. WHITE. I can see you.

JENNINGS. Yes, but can you hear us?

MS. WHITE. Can I hear you?

JENNINGS. CAN YOU HEAR US?

MR. PAINE. CAN YOU HEAR US, OR JUST SEE US?

MS. WHITE. I can both see and hear you.

JENNINGS. Excellent.

MS. WHITE. Wait – do you hear that?

JENNINGS. No.

MR. PAINE. Hear what, White?

MS. WHITE. The pitter-patter.

JENNINGS. There is a pitter-patter?

MS. WHITE. Is there a shower here?

MR. PAINE. No shower, White.

MS. WHITE. That's a shame really, I thought I heard the shower.

JENNINGS. Yes. The pitter-patter.

MS. WHITE. There was a small, brief pitter-patter, but – now it's gone.

JENNINGS. Things do disappear.

>   (Beat.)

MS. WHITE. Did you just ask if that chair's taken?

JENNINGS. That chair?

MS. WHITE. Yes, ask if it's been taken?

MR. PAINE. As in – excuse me, is that chair taken?

MS. WHITE. Yes.

JENNINGS. How would we know if that chair's taken?

MR. PAINE. But what chair? There is no chair.

>   (There is no chair.)

MS. WHITE. It's just that I heard the question –

JENNINGS. I could've sworn I'd seen a chair –

MS. WHITE. Perhaps it's been taken?

JENNINGS. If the chair that is in question was here a moment ago, and you heard someone ask if it's been taken, perhaps it was that same person that took the chair? Clearly they were interested in the chair, had a use for it, a need. I'm sure that's where it went.

MS. WHITE. Of course.

JENNINGS. What's more pressing to me, is this matter of time.

MS. WHITE. We're being timed, yes.

MR. PAINE. I'm sure of it.

JENNINGS. We know we're being timed, we've been told that, but I want to know HOW we are being timed. Are they timing us quickly? Are they timing us in increments?

MR. PAINE. Can they time us quickly?

JENNINGS. They can do whatever they want, Paine! They already took the chair.

MS. WHITE. Jennings, grab hold! Time is not something that they can do quickly to us –

JENNINGS. I've seen it happen.

MS. WHITE. No.

MR. PAINE. When?

JENNINGS. They've been known to speed it up. I was there.

MS. WHITE. There?

JENNINGS. In the room when it happened.

MR. PAINE. Was the room...white?

JENNINGS. If this is The White Room, how could that room also be white.

MS. WHITE. What did it look like?

JENNINGS. I'll try to explain. It might be easier if I show you, not everything has words to describe it.

(JENNINGS *does the time lapse movement piece. It happens fairly quickly.*)

MS. WHITE. Fascinating! I never knew it was possible –

MR. PAINE. Can we, well, help move time along? Do we have any power over how quickly it happens?

JENNINGS. If you were watching carefully, you'd have seen that I did help time move along more quickly towards the middle. I'd realized what was happening and it was natural for me to put my hands behind my back at a certain point and go with it.

MR. PAINE. I thought it was nice when you did that.

JENNINGS. It was necessary, not nice.

MS. WHITE. They are not exclusive of each other – something can be both nice and necessary.

MR. PAINE. What color was the room, Jennings?

JENNINGS. That room actually didn't have a color. I highly doubt it was even a room. So, you can see my concern over the way in which we are being timed.

MS. WHITE. It seems to me, if we make an effort to not have our hands behind our back ever, we will be timed in the traditional fashion.

JENNINGS. It couldn't hurt, but I'm not sure it would help.

MR. PAINE. Well, talking about it doesn't help. It's a waste.

MS. WHITE. It's a waste of time, you're right.

MR. PAINE. Caution. That's what the fish's mouth had mouthed. Caution.

MS. WHITE. Now, who is feeling something?

> *(Beat.)*

Any urge to kiss me, Mr. Paine?

MR. PAINE. None.

MS. WHITE. Jennings?

JENNINGS. No thank you.

MS. WHITE. Any wants?

JENNINGS. I'm feeling a bit full, from the cards.

MR. PAINE. Yes, bit tired. But one thing leads to another and eating has led to tiredness. I remember the first time I was aware that one thing leads to another. I was on the dock, it was night, they had just left.

MS. WHITE. The night of The Big Clean?

MR. PAINE. It was the night of The Big Clean.

> *(He clucks.)*

I had followed them down to the dock, hoping they'd drop something. They did not. I slowly made my way up to the house and as I walked inside I noticed something immediately. Nothing was there. There was an emptiness.

JENNINGS. Absence?

MR. PAINE. There was emptiness and absence. I crawled up on the only thing left, the couch, and stayed there.

MS. WHITE. Was it a fold out couch?

MR. PAINE. No, it had three cushions, a strange synthetic material that was rough on the cheek, threads of green and brown, buttons that rubbed on your back.

JENNINGS. I'm so sorry, Paine.

MR. PAINE. I was sorry, too. But one thing led to another and I still had the couch. I was so small, not ready to embrace an absence.

MS. WHITE. Unfair.

MR. PAINE. No fairness.

(**MR. PAINE**'s *arm starts to rise again.*)

MS. WHITE. Mr. Paine, your arm again.

MR. PAINE. Why yes! There it goes.

JENNINGS. Ms. White, I'm not sure you heard us before, but I hope you'll agree that I'm quite sure that Mr. Paine can not fly.

MR. PAINE. Shame.

MS. WHITE. I am sorry to hear that, Paine, it's nice to fly, to be up so high.

MR. PAINE. I'll never know.

MS. WHITE. I can tell you. I can show you. Very slowly lift yourself off the ground, control your flapping, keep focused.

MR. PAINE. I'm trying… Flying must not be for everyone.

JENNINGS. Certainly not. You could cry, though, Paine, I bet that's something you could do.

MR. PAINE. You think?

MS. WHITE. You could cry.

MR. PAINE. Would it be hard?

MS. WHITE. It might.

JENNINGS. But you should try. If you're convinced on doing something, it just might fit.

MR. PAINE. Okay.

JENNINGS. Are you crying yet?

MR. PAINE. Not yet.

MS. WHITE. Now?

MR. PAINE. No.

MS. WHITE. It might take a moment.

(They wait.)

JENNINGS. Now?

MR. PAINE. Almost.

MS. WHITE. I want to help –

JENNINGS. Yes, let's help Paine cry.

MR. PAINE. Well, there is something that might help. Ms. White, I hesitate to even ask, but, do you mind repeating after me?

MS. WHITE. Repeating after me?

MR. PAINE. Exactly!

MS. WHITE. Exactly!

MR. PAINE. Poo Poo, you know why you're in my office.

MS. WHITE. Poo Poo, you know why you're in my office.

MR. PAINE. And it's precisely because of that that you're here.

MS. WHITE. And it's precisely because of that that you're here.

JENNINGS. Nice going… I think you're almost there –

MR. PAINE. AND, we'll not stand for that any more, especially from someone like you.

MS. WHITE. AND, we'll not stand for that any more, especially from someone like you.

JENNINGS. Heavens no.

(MR. PAINE starts crying.)

MS. WHITE. That's right –

JENNINGS. You're almost –

MS. WHITE. He's there.

JENNINGS. I knew you could do it.

(MR. PAINE is sobbing; he picks up the negligee.)

MR. PAINE. Ms. White?

MS. WHITE. Yes?

MR. PAINE. Will you please –

JENNINGS. Oh – pretty please –

MR. PAINE. Put it on?

MS. WHITE. It did come through the door.

JENNINGS. I can light the candles, it'll be like a party.

MR. PAINE. *(Sniffling.)* Will there be guests?

JENNINGS. I don't see how.

MS. WHITE. I don't see how either. If I put the dress on, and we light the candles and have the party, we have to keep our objectives in mind, have to constantly be thinking about why we are here and what we are doing –

JENNINGS. What are we doing?

> *(They are silent for a moment.)*

MS. WHITE. We are solving.

JENNINGS. They must know what they're doing. They want us to have this party, as motivation –

MR. PAINE. They're rewarding us –

MS. WHITE. Rewarding us, yes. You will be rewarded along the way.

MR. PAINE. We're having a party!

JENNINGS. Can we discuss all this at the party?

> *(MR. PAINE tosses the negligee to MS. WHITE.)*

MS. WHITE. Alright. Jennings – light the candles, I'll dress behind the pedestal. Paine – no peeking.

MR. PAINE. What –

MS. WHITE. Paine.

MR. PAINE. I need a job. You both have jobs. I would like to contribute to the party.

JENNINGS. Well, you can work on the Entertainment Portion.

MR. PAINE. The Entertainment Portion!

JENNINGS. Brilliant, a party!

> *(MS. WHITE goes behind the pedestal to change, MR. PAINE sits cross-legged in Creative Meditation Mode, and JENNINGS lines the three votive candles up and is in position to strike the match.)*

PART FOUR – THE PARTY THAT HAPPENS BECAUSE OF THE PACKAGE THAT CAME THROUGH THE SLOT IN THE DOOR TO THE WHITE ROOM

(**MS. WHITE** *has changed into the negligee.* **MR. PAINE** *continues his Entertainment Meditation, and* **JENNINGS** *strikes the match.*)

(*On lighting it, the lights dim, and the slow rise of The Tango Music. It underscores the scene, ebbing and flowing with preciseness to the dialogue.*)

(**JENNINGS** *lights the candles and the mood is set. They all convene near the pedestal and are in the positions they were in at the top of the show. They bow to each other as if at some ancient, formal party.*)

MS. WHITE. Ms. White.

MR. PAINE. Ah, Ms. White.

JENNINGS. Ms. White.

MS. WHITE. You...

JENNINGS. Jennings.

MS. WHITE. Jennings.

MR. PAINE. Ah, Jennings. Mr. Paine.

MS. WHITE. Mr. Paine.

JENNINGS. Mr. Paine, your reputation precedes you.

MR. PAINE. As does yours.

MS. WHITE. And yours.

MR. PAINE. And yours.

JENNINGS. And yours.

MS. WHITE. And yours.

(*Beat.*)

Who will dance?

JENNINGS. Mr. Paine?

MS. WHITE. Mr. Paine?

MR. PAINE. Ms. White.

JENNINGS. Ms. White.

MS. WHITE. Very well.

MR. PAINE. Jennings – for the Entertainment Portion of the party, I will dance with Ms. White as you spin a tale of some sort.

JENNINGS. A tale?

MR. PAINE. To the music. You are the narrator and we, the destined to die after one dance – star-crossed lovers that met on the balcony overlooking the sea for one last sad, lover-like tango.

JENNINGS. Ms. White?

MS. WHITE. Jennings?

JENNINGS. Are you sure?

MS. WHITE. It seems appropriate, it is a party.

JENNINGS. But are we…off-course?

MS. WHITE. Course, Jennings?

MR. PAINE. How would we know?

MS. WHITE. *(Laughing.)* We can't possibly know if we're on-course or off-course.

MR. PAINE. The course hasn't been set.

MS. WHITE. We are the course.

MR. PAINE. This sets the course.

JENNINGS. Of course. Put your gloves on, Paine.

MR. PAINE. Gloves?

JENNINGS. In your pocket.

> **(MR. PAINE** *reaches into his pocket and pulls out a pair of men's dress gloves. He puts them on.)*

Ask her to dance.

MR. PAINE. May I have this dance.

MS. WHITE. You may.

JENNINGS. Tell her how beautiful she looks, Paine.

MR. PAINE. You are stunning.

MS. WHITE. *(Blushing.)* Thank you. What nice gloves.

(**MR. PAINE** *leads her onto The Dance Floor. They begin The Tango.*)

JENNINGS. This isn't the first time you have danced… Not the first time your gloved hand has fit so perfectly with hers as you lead her across the floor.

MR. PAINE. We danced on the dock –

JENNINGS. You danced on the dock, under the crescent moon.

MS. WHITE. It was just a sliver really, a small sliver –

JENNINGS. A whisper of a moon.

MS. WHITE. My favorite moon.

JENNINGS. Take her more firmly, Paine.

(**MR. PAINE** *takes her more firmly.*)

She wasn't yours to have that night on the dock, was she.

(*Beat.*)

What is it about this dock of yours, Paine?

MR. PAINE. Jennings! We've barely started dancing –

JENNINGS. She wasn't yours to have that night on the dock, but you danced with her anyway didn't you. With abandon. You took her by her child waist and twirled her and stared into her eyes –

(**MS. WHITE** *clearly mouths the word CAUTION.*)

– it was an eye lock that would never, ever end, that you had not thought possible, that you had only heard about –

MR. PAINE. Caution –

JENNINGS. Through eternity. Your cheek brushed hers –

(**MS. WHITE** *lets out a small sigh.*)

And a magnificent flood of light framed her from behind – she was glowing, ethereal and slightly dangerous.

MS. WHITE. I've always dreamed of being dangerous!

JENNINGS. Slightly dangerous, her lips full red, her legs long as the day, her eye lock never ending.

MR. PAINE. I'd had chicken for dinner that night –

MS. WHITE. Dangerous to the touch –

(*MR. PAINE clucks like a chicken.*)

JENNINGS. The halo of light didn't fool you –

MR. PAINE. There was broccoli on the side –

JENNINGS. You led her close to the edge, the water shimmering in the whisper-less sliver of the moon –

MS. WHITE. Reflected in my eyes!

(*MR. PAINE clucks like a chicken.*)

JENNINGS. The moon was reflected –

MS. WHITE. – glinting even, as we stared at each other –

MR. PAINE. Something's caught in my teeth –

MS. WHITE. I'm feeling –

MR. PAINE. What is that –

MS. WHITE. – feeling toxically emotional.

MR. PAINE. Broccoli?

JENNINGS. You dip her down –

MR. PAINE. I believe there is broccoli in my teeth!

JENNINGS. – her hair grazing the waters, the wetness grazing the hair –

MS. WHITE. The wetness…

MR. PAINE. It's all so clear –

MS. WHITE. It's the perfect night –

JENNINGS. What are you feeling, Paine?

MR. PAINE. (*He has the strongest desire to kiss her.*) No –

JENNINGS. What are you seeing –

MR. PAINE. Not again –

(*He clucks.*)

MS. WHITE. Hold me –

MR. PAINE. I'm holding you.

JENNINGS. You are holding each other!

MR. PAINE. Oh no –

JENNINGS. Oh no?

MS. WHITE. Oh no…

MR. PAINE. I want to kiss you –

MS. WHITE. No…

MR. PAINE. I'm leaning –

JENNINGS. And listing –

MR. PAINE. But, I –

JENNINGS. You what, Paine?

MS. WHITE. I –

JENNINGS. You?

MS. WHITE. You can't!

MR. PAINE. I can't!

(They are twirling; the music is soaring.)

JENNINGS. To truly feel alive, to burn, to feel both rare and divine – to know what it's like the moment before flight – is to know –

MR. PAINE. Is to know –

MS. WHITE. Yes, is to know the moment before –

JENNINGS. A sharp intake of breath –

MS. WHITE. A micro moment prior –

MR. PAINE. Complete awareness and abandon –

MS. WHITE. Just before –

JENNINGS. The moment before death!

*(The music abruptly stops; lights shift back to normal – perhaps slightly brighter than before. Suddenly, the door with the slot in it opens, and **PATRICK** is hurled into the room, crashing into the pedestal, and landing on the floor.)*

PART FIVE – THE END OF THE PARTY THAT HAPPENS BECAUSE OF THE PACKAGE THAT CAME THROUGH THE SLOT IN THE DOOR TO THE WHITE ROOM

(PATRICK *slowly rises. He has a note pinned to him. They all stare.*)

MR. PAINE. Is the party over?

JENNINGS. Pretty sure, Paine.

MR. PAINE. Were we dancing?

MS. WHITE. We were dancing.

MR. PAINE. We had a good time, didn't we Ms. White, when we danced?

MS. WHITE. I remember, yes.

JENNINGS. You made a stunning couple.

(*Noticing something hanging out of* **MR. PAINE**'*s coat.*)

Paine – what's that hanging out of your coat?

MR. PAINE. What?

JENNINGS. In the back, that purple thing.

(**MR. PAINE** *pulls The Purple Rope out of his coat.*)

MS. WHITE. The Purple Rope.

MR. PAINE. The Purple Rope!

JENNINGS. Indeed.

MS. WHITE. (*Nodding to* **PATRICK**.) Do you see him?

JENNINGS. Yes.

MR. PAINE. Yes.

MS. WHITE. Do you see that note pinned to him?

(*Beat.*)

Mr. Paine, will you get the note?

(**MR. PAINE** *retrieves the note.*)

MR. PAINE. Blank. Jennings?

JENNINGS. Blank.

MS. WHITE. Let me see it. It's not blank.

(*Reading from the note.*)

"His name is Patrick. Patrick's upbringing was normal. Parents that loved him. Girls that called him. Teachers that bragged about him. He's never been hungry. Never been hit. Never had to go to bed early. Without any supper."

(**PATRICK** *gently takes the note from* **MS. WHITE** *and begins to read.*)

PATRICK. "He is twenty-eight years old and has not been out of his apartment since he was fourteen. That's half of Patrick's life. The concept of sunrise and sunset holds no other image than a burst of pixels on a screen."

(*Laughs.*)

Love it. "He urinates through a tube that runs from the toilet to his pants as he sits on the couch."

It's thirty-four feet long, Jennings. It's genius – "brilliant" as you'd say. I love it when you say that, how you say that. Goddamn Brits man – crack me up. You'd love the forethought. Bathroom's all the way down the hall, time saver.

"He is capable of precisely six emotions: want, yearning, contentment, tiredness, hunger, and anticipation. These are the same six emotions felt by children under six. Patrick has never been on a boat (though he has been on a dock), has not ridden in a car or flown in a plane, has never felt the soft touch of a caring hand and has never been kissed.

In order for Patrick to win, you must make him want it. To win it, to sacrifice for it. But first you must wake Patrick up from his virtual slumber."

Virtual slumber… Love it.

(**PATRICK** *walks slowly around the room, sizing it up. He takes his time with each of them.*)

Ms. White – you're prettier than I'd ever imagined. I thought you'd be smaller somehow and more translucent looking – but you're so pretty. And so smart. I've wanted to select you for a long, long time. Your hair is so shiny –

(He touches her hair.)

And, Jennings, my mate, you are one funny guy. One. Funny. Guy. Max and I'll be sitting there, and we won't have said a word for hours – not for hours – once, it got so intense Max did not talk for thirty-three days. But you'll come on or be in a room or something and we'll holler! We'll holler we're so excited – because you crack us up. Crack. Us. Up.

(He turns to **MR. PAINE.**)

Paine, FUCK! I've had you the longest. Couple years now. All the way back to the aquatic, do you remember? CAUTION. I love your brain man, how it just knows all this shit, you know? Everything.

And you guys are all so fucking deep! I love it. I would NEVER have thought of this shit.

Jennings, brilliant man, the whole kiss thing, how you all just, you know, figured out that not kissing was what you were supposed to do, that counter instinct instinct reversal stuff.

Paine – the boar's saliva spread-eagle mating position, I almost fell off the goddamn couch, tube almost popped out and I would've just pissed myself. Seriously, almost pissed myself.

So, this is it, huh? White, never would have thought that the final room was white. Seems blandish after everything we've been through, doesn't it? So what now?

(Beat.)

How do we do it? I assume that's what you guys have been doing right?

MS. WHITE. Doing?

PATRICK. While I was getting here.

MS. WHITE. Jennings – were we doing that?

JENNINGS. I suppose so. Mr. Paine, right?

MR. PAINE. Seems right.

PATRICK. So?

MR. PAINE. Yes.

PATRICK. How do we get out?

MS. WHITE. Out?

JENNINGS. Ahhhh. Out. That's the objective.

MS. WHITE. The game.

JENNINGS. Of course.

MS. WHITE. Patrick. Do you mind if we conference?

PATRICK. Conference away – but hurry –

JENNINGS. – The time thing, yes.

PATRICK. I picked up a bit more just before I got here, but, you know…

MS. WHITE. Of course. Paine? Jennings?

> (**MS. WHITE, MR. PAINE,** *and* **JENNINGS** *huddle in a corner to regroup.*)

PATRICK. And that tango! That. Was. Great. Everyone was talking about it. Hot, hot, hot.

> (*He tangos solo across the floor.*)

It was getting so heated for a minute… Paine – you're wacked dude – you kept slipping back to The Big Clean. I shudder just thinking about that. I was almost out for good. I should be dead. I was so close, do you remember how close I was? If I hadn't seen The Purple Rope, I'd of been a goner for sure.

You guys! Did you know that I'm, we're, currently, the A Number One Player In All Of History? All. Of. History. Damn! We get out of this room and it's over.

> (*Beat. They un-huddle and approach* **PATRICK.**)

MS. WHITE. Patrick.

PATRICK. Ms. White.

MS. WHITE. Patrick, are you on your couch right now?

PATRICK. Yeah.

> (**JENNINGS**, **MR. PAINE**, *and* **MS. WHITE** *exchange a look.*)

JENNINGS. We thought so. Excellent.

MS. WHITE. Are you home alone? Or are there other people there.

PATRICK. Max is here. Of course.

MS. WHITE. Sitting next to you?

PATRICK. Yes.

MR. PAINE. Right or left side?

PATRICK. Right.

JENNINGS. Patrick, we've regrouped, just now, as you saw, in that corner. We examined the tools we possess, why you have chosen us, what we bring, and how we complement each other. We can get you out of here.

PATRICK. Perfect!

JENNINGS. What we have been discussing is hard to put into words, traditional words that you will understand –

MR. PAINE. Did we have chicken for dinner, Patrick?

PATRICK. With broccoli, man.

MR. PAINE. Thought so.

MS. WHITE. What Jennings is trying to explain –

JENNINGS. What I am trying to explain is that we have regrouped –

MS. WHITE. Decoded if you will and we believe we know what must happen for you to get out. It's a bit, well, tricky.

MR. PAINE. Tricky.

JENNINGS. Tricky.

> (*Beat.*)

Is Max still sitting next to you, Patrick?

PATRICK. We do not, ever, get up.

MR. PAINE. Patrick, now you have to trust us with this. Clear your mind. We have been in here, as you know, discussing this exact thing for some time. But, since it seems we are an extension of you –

MS. WHITE. That you selected us –

MR. PAINE. There are parts of us that –

JENNINGS. – that pick up on your thoughts – and this, often, interrupts our mission. You must trust us.

MS. WHITE. Completely.

PATRICK. I do, I will, anything.

MS. WHITE. No thinking of when you were a child genius of six, or the girls you never kissed, or the dinner caught in your teeth.

JENNINGS. We keep the objective simple.

MS. WHITE. Simple.

MR. PAINE. Simple.

MS. WHITE. We have weighed both science and nature –

MR. PAINE. Have struck a bargain with logic –

MS. WHITE. And we have found the loophole.

MR. PAINE. There is a loophole.

JENNINGS. It is a brilliant loophole.

PATRICK. Brilliant!

JENNINGS. Opponents… Max sits next to you on the couch, he is in the game too, isn't he?

PATRICK. Behind me though –

MR. PAINE. But gaining, I'm sure.

JENNINGS. Opponents! We need to feed off this opposing energy.

MS. WHITE. Full Experience varies from person to person, player to player –

MR. PAINE. The answers will just pop in your mind, once we clear it.

MS. WHITE. Jennings, explain the course.

JENNINGS. To exit the room, more energy is needed than you possess, than we collectively possess.

We need Max.

MS. WHITE. Eliminated.

MR. PAINE. Out.

MS. WHITE. Do you understand?

PATRICK. I think so…

MS. WHITE. What is Max doing now?

PATRICK. Sitting here, playing, breathing too loud.

MS. WHITE. Mr. Paine.

>   (**MR. PAINE** *hands his gloves and The Purple Rope*
>   *to* **PATRICK.**)

Put the gloves on, Patrick, fasten the rope around your waist. Jennings?

>   (**JENNINGS** *lights the candles again, and like*
>   *before, with the striking of the match the lights shift*
>   *and The Tango Music starts, softly.*)

PATRICK. Party?

MS. WHITE. Just do as we ask, Patrick.

PATRICK. Anything you say, Ms. White.

MR. PAINE. You're the Jack of Spades, Patrick –

PATRICK. Damn straight, favorite card.

MS. WHITE. Exactly. Come here.

>   (**PATRICK** *goes to* **MS. WHITE**; *they start dancing*
>   *The Tango. The music builds and they dance*
>   *through the following, to the end.*)

Listen to the methodical tugging of Jennings' voice, Patrick…

JENNINGS. Max is to your right on the sofa. He is breathing a little too loudly. We need that breath. Stare into Ms. White's eyes. You twirl with her, there are whispers –

>   (**JENNINGS** *and* **MR. PAINE** *circle around them as*
>   *they dance.*)

Patrick – reach over and jokingly punch Max on the shoulder as you dip Ms. White.

(PATRICK dips MS. WHITE.)

PATRICK. He didn't like that.

JENNINGS. Good.

MR. PAINE. Max is smaller than you, isn't he, Patrick?

PATRICK. Yes.

MS. WHITE. It's the perfect night –

JENNINGS. Hit his controller out of his hand.

PATRICK. What?

MS. WHITE. Patrick you are so strong –

JENNINGS. Hit his controller out of his hand.

MS. WHITE. I've never been held in arms like yours –

PATRICK. Done.

MR. PAINE. In one quick, sharp move – throw Max onto the ground and pin his arms under your shins as you sit on him.

PATRICK. Really?

MS. WHITE. Do it.

PATRICK. Done.

(They are twirling; the music is soaring.)

MS. WHITE. I have the strongest desire to kiss you, Patrick –

JENNINGS. Hurry, Patrick –

MR. PAINE. Faster –

PATRICK. He's yelling –

JENNINGS. Make sure he can't move –

PATRICK. He's not going anywhere.

MR. PAINE. Hold her firmly, Patrick –

PATRICK. Yes –

JENNINGS. Keep him pinned, Patrick –

PATRICK. Yes –

JENNINGS. Breathe in the energy of the struggle –

MS. WHITE. Do you want to kiss me, Patrick?

PATRICK. I...do –

MR. PAINE. Use that desire –

JENNINGS. Is there a pillow on the couch next to you, Patrick –

PATRICK. There are two.

(*To* MS. WHITE.)

You are stunning.

MS. WHITE. Thank you. What nice gloves.

MR. PAINE. Grab the pillow closest to you.

PATRICK. Okay –

JENNINGS. We are very close now –

PATRICK. He's crying –

JENNINGS. Patrick –

PATRICK. And struggling –

(*The frame of The Door in the room starts glowing.*)

JENNINGS. The Door –

PATRICK. I can't –

MS. WHITE. You must.

JENNINGS. We only need it open, there is a small window, the adrenaline –

MR. PAINE. Put the pillow over Max's face.

JENNINGS. To feel truly alive –

MS. WHITE. Do you want to truly feel alive, Patrick?

PATRICK. I do –

JENNINGS. To know what it's like –

MR. PAINE. To harvest that energy –

JENNINGS. The moment before –

MR. PAINE. The only way to get out.

PATRICK. The pillow is on his face.

(*They are twirling; the music is soaring.*)

Max is kicking.

MR. PAINE. Press it down.

JENNINGS. Breathe him in.

(*The door is rattling.*)

MS. WHITE. Hold me tight.

PATRICK. We're almost –

JENNINGS. Time this right –

PATRICK. I've got him down –

JENNINGS. The moment before –

MS. WHITE. The exact moment before –

JENNINGS. You will dive through the door.

PATRICK. Ms. White has a halo behind her –

JENNINGS. It is the only passage –

MR. PAINE. Feel him through that pillow, Patrick –

PATRICK. I have him…

MR. PAINE. When you know it's the last sharp intake –

JENNINGS. The last gulp –

MS. WHITE. The kinetic transcendency –

JENNINGS. When you know it's right – fly through that door.

PATRICK. It's so close –

JENNINGS. Keep him down –

PATRICK. I can feel it.

MR. PAINE. Hold her tight –

MS. WHITE. To truly feel alive –

MR. PAINE. To know what it's like –

MS. WHITE. It's the only way out –

JENNINGS. Is to know the moment –

MS. WHITE. The moment –

MR. PAINE. The moment –

JENNINGS. Just before death –

> *(The Door opens and* **PATRICK** *dives through. It flutters momentarily and then shuts.)*

End of Play